Merry Christmas
Baby

Love The Buckan's

THIS IS A BORZOI BOOK PUBLISHED BY ALFRED A. KNOPF

Illustrations copyright © 1984 by Anita Lobel
All rights reserved under International and Pan-American Copyright Conventions.
Published in the United States by Alfred A. Knopf, an imprint of Random House
Children's Books, a division of Random House, Inc., New York, and simultaneously
in Canada by Random House of Canada Limited, Toronto. Distributed by Random
House, Inc., New York. Originally published in hardcover as a
Borzoi Book by Alfred A. Knopf, a division of Random House, Inc.,
in 1984 and as a paperback by Dragonfly Books in 1988.
www.randomhouse.com/kids
KNOPF, BORZOI BOOKS, and the colophon are registered trademarks of
Random House, Inc.

Library of Congress Cataloging-in-Publication Data
Moore, Clement Clarke, 1779–1863. The night before Christmas.
Summary: A well-known poem about an important Christmas Eve visitor.
1. Santa Claus—Juvenile poetry. 2. Christmas—Juvenile poetry. 3. Children's poetry,
American. [1. Santa Claus—Poetry. 2. Christmas—Poetry. 3. American poetry.
4. Narrative poetry.] I. Lobel, Anita, ill. II. Title.
PS2429.M5N5   1984   811'.2   84-4342
ISBN 0-375-82414-6 (trade)
ISBN 0-375-92414-0 (lib. bdg.)
ISBN 0-375-81047-1 (pbk.)

Printed in Singapore
September 2003
10 9 8 7 6 5 4 3

The Night Before CHRISTMAS

Written by
Clement C. Moore

Illustrated by
Anita Lobel

Alfred A. Knopf · New York

’T was the night before Christmas,
when all through the house
not a creature was stirring,
not even a mouse;

The stockings were hung by the chimney with care,
In hopes that St. Nicholas soon would be there;

The children were nestled all snug in their beds
While visions of sugar plums danced in their heads;

And Mamma in her kerchief, and I in my cap,
Had just settled our brains for a long winter's nap,

When out on the lawn there arose such a clatter,
I sprang from my bed to see what was the matter.
Away to the window I flew like a flash,
Tore open the shutters and threw up the sash.
The moon on the breast of the new-fallen snow
Gave a lustre of midday to objects below,
When, what to my wondering eyes should appear,
But a miniature sleigh and eight tiny reindeer,
With a little old driver, so lively and quick,
I knew in a moment it must be St. Nick.

More rapid than eagles his coursers they came,
And he whistled, and shouted, and called them by name:
"Now, Dasher! now, Dancer! now, Prancer and Vixen!
On, Comet! on, Cupid! on, Donder and Blitzen!
To the top of the porch! to the top of the wall!
Now dash away! dash away! dash away, all!"

As dry leaves that before the wild hurricane fly,
When they meet with an obstacle, mount to the sky,
So up to the housetop the coursers they flew,
With a sleigh full of toys, and St. Nicholas, too.

And then, in a twinkling, I heard on the roof
The prancing and pawing of each little hoof.

As I drew in my head, and was turning around,
Down the chimney St. Nicholas came with a bound.
He was dressed all in fur, from his head to his foot,
And his clothes were all tarnished with ashes and soot;
A bundle of toys he had flung on his back,
And he looked like a peddler just opening his pack.
His eyes—how they twinkled! his dimples, how merry!
His cheeks were like roses, his nose like a cherry!
His droll little mouth was drawn up like a bow,
And the beard on his chin was as white as the snow;
The stump of a pipe he held tight in his teeth,
And the smoke, it encircled his head like a wreath;
He had a broad face and a little round belly
That shook, when he laughed, like a bowl full of jelly.
He was chubby and plump, a right jolly old elf,
And I laughed when I saw him, in spite of myself;
A wink of his eye and a twist of his head,
Soon gave me to know I had nothing to dread;

He spoke not a word, but went straight to his work,
And filled all the stockings; then turned with a jerk,

And laying a finger aside of his nose,
And giving a nod, up the chimney he rose.

He sprang to his sleigh, to his team gave a whistle,
And away they all flew like the down of a thistle.
But I heard him exclaim, ere he drove out of sight,

"Happy Christmas to all,
And to all a good night!"